Scum

Scum

James C. Dekker

orca soundings

ORCA BOOK PUBLISHERS

Copyright © 2008 James C. Dekker

All rights reserved. No part of this publication may be reproduced or transmitted in any form or by any means, electronic or mechanical, including photocopying, recording or by any information storage and retrieval system now known or to be invented, without permission in writing from the publisher.

Library and Archives Canada Cataloguing in Publication

Dekker, James C.
Scum / James C. Dekker.
(Orca soundings)

ISBN 978-1-55143-926-6 (bound).--ISBN 978-1-55143-924-2 (PBK.)

I. Title. II. Series.
PS8607.E4825S38 2008   jC813'.6   C2008-903105-9

First published in the United States, 2008
Library of Congress Control Number: 2008928741

Summary: Fifteen-year-old Megan's brother is dead, apparently a random victim of violence. As Megan digs deeper, she finds that Danny was "known to police" and that nobody wants to solve the crime.

Orca Book Publishers is dedicated to preserving the environment and has printed this book on paper certified by the Forest Stewardship Council®.

Orca Book Publishers gratefully acknowledges the support for its publishing programs provided by the following agencies: the Government of Canada through the Canada Book Fund and the Canada Council for the Arts, and the Province of British Columbia through the BC Arts Council and the Book Publishing Tax Credit.

Cover photography by Getty Images

ORCA BOOK PUBLISHERS
PO Box 5626, Stn. B
Victoria, BC Canada
V8R 6S4

ORCA BOOK PUBLISHERS
PO Box 468
Custer, WA USA
98240-0468

www.orcabook.com
Printed and bound in Canada.

14 13 12 11 • 5 4 3 2

Chapter One

Every time it's my birthday or my brother Danny's birthday, my mother always says the same thing. She always says, "I remember the day you were born like it was yesterday. I remember when they put you in my arms. I'll never forget."

Here's a day I'll never forget.

Seven thirty Friday morning. My dad is sitting at the kitchen table with his newspaper and his cup of coffee. My mom is at the stove making eggs for me. I don't like eggs. But I'm a vegetarian, so my mother makes me eat them so that I'll get enough protein. The doorbell rings. My dad frowns slightly as he looks over the top of his paper at me. My mom turns from the stove and nods at me. Right. Go answer the door, Megan.

So I go. As I walk from the kitchen at the back of the house down the hall toward the front door, I wonder who it could be. It's way too early for it to be Caitlin or Shannon. We don't hook up until at least eight fifteen to walk to school. Maybe Caitlin had another fight with her mother. When that happens, she comes to my house and we go up to my room and she tells me—again—how she can't wait until the end of next year when she finishes high school, how the only universities she's going to apply to are going to be clear across the country, so far away that she'll only have to see her mother on holidays, assuming she even decides to go home.

But it isn't Caitlin at the door.

It's two men in suits. One is tall and bulky. He looks like he could be a wrestler, except what would a wrestler be doing at our door at seven thirty in the morning? The other one is shorter and wiry. They both have serious expressions on their faces. The shorter one says, "Is your father or mother at home?"

"They both are," I say.

Behind me, I hear my mother yell, "Who is it, Megan?"

So I call back to her, "There's someone here who wants to talk to you or Dad." I turn back to look at the two men, who are standing silent on the porch. The shorter one glances up at the taller one.

Then my mother comes down the hall, an apron over her skirt and silk blouse. She is district manager of a chain of video stores. She believes in dressing for success. She nudges me aside and looks at the two men in suits. I don't know for sure, but from the look on her face I think maybe she thinks they're Jehovah's Witnesses or something like that, here to try to save her.

"Mrs. Carter?" the shorter man says.

Surprise registers on my mother's face, and I realize they can't be Jehovah's Witnesses. They know her name. Suddenly I get the feeling that something is wrong.

"Are you related to Daniel Carter?" the shorter man says.

That's when it hits me. These guys are cops. I can't count the number of times I have told Danny how stupid he is. I can't count the number of times I've told him, One of these days you're going to get busted. I can't count the number of times I've told him, What do you think Mom's going to do when the cops show up at the front door asking questions about you?

But you can't tell Danny anything. You never could. The company he keeps—he thinks he's smarter and tougher and faster than anyone else, especially the cops. But here they are, at our door, just like I told him they would be one day. And now Mom's about to find out what Danny's been up to, and it's going to kill her.

My mother is frowning. She knows that something's wrong. She says, "He's my son. Why? What's this all about?"

I think it's about Danny finally getting busted. It's about him not being as smart and as tough and as fast as he thinks. It's about the cops not being as dumb and as slow as he always makes them out to be.

I hear a shuffling sound behind me. It's my dad, still in his slippers, the newspaper still in his hands. He's coming to see what's going on. At first he has a kind of puzzled, half-there expression on his face. My dad is an architect. When he's working on a new project, you always get the feeling that he's somewhere else, deep inside his head, seeing things that don't exist because he hasn't created them yet. But when he sees the two men in suits at the door, suddenly he's right there. He looks at me. He's probably thinking the same thing I am.

"What's going on?" he says.

My mother glances over her shoulder at him. "It's something about Danny," she says.

The shorter man has pulled something out of his pocket. It's his identification. I knew it. He's a cop.

Chapter Two

At first my mother doesn't seem to understand. Why are there cops at our house? Why are they talking about Danny?

"Where is he?" she says. "Is he all right?"

The taller cop looks down at his partner. I have this weird feeling that they tossed a coin before they rang our doorbell—the loser gets to tell the family.

"Was he in an accident?" my mother says.

I glance at my father. His face is somber. He is bracing himself for bad news.

"I'm sorry to have to tell you this, Mrs. Carter," the shorter cop says, "but he's been shot."

"Shot?" My mother looks stunned. She shakes her head. Then, just for a second, I see the hint of a smile on her face, like she thinks this must be a joke. "No," she says. "That's not possible." She sounds so positive. "You've made a mistake."

"Your son is Daniel Christopher Carter," the shorter cop says.

"Yes," my mother says, confused and alarmed. I can see it in her eyes. "Yes, that's my son. He's been *shot*?" It's like she can't believe it. "Is he all right?"

"I'm sorry," the shorter cop says. "He's dead."

My mother stares at the cop. My father touches her elbow. He tries to pull her gently back into the house, but she won't move.

"No," she says. "No."

My father finally manages to ease her inside. When the two cops come into the house, I see one of our neighbors standing on the sidewalk, looking up at me. Another neighbor goes up to him and says something. The first neighbor shakes his head. They both look at our house. I close the door.

My father is asking the two cops to wait, please just wait a minute, he wants to attend to his wife. He takes her into the living room and makes her sit down on the couch. He gives her some tissues. He tells her he'll be right back. He tells me to go and sit with my mother. When I hesitate—I want to know what happened—he tells me, "Go, Meggie." As I start to go to my mother, I hear my father say to the cops, "Please, there are some things my wife doesn't know."

In fact, there are a lot of things she doesn't know.

My mother stops crying when I come into the room. She sees my father talking in a low voice to the two cops out in the front hall. She stands up. She says, "What's going on, Paul?"

"I'm just having a word with these two detectives," my father says.

"I want to know what happened," my mother says. "I want to know what happened to Danny."

The shorter cop looks at my father for a moment. Then he comes into the living room. He introduces himself as Detective Rossetti, homicide. His partner, the big cop who looks like a wrestler, is Detective French. Detective Rossetti asks my mother if she minds if he sits down. My mother says she doesn't mind. She sits too.

Detective Rossetti says, "Danny was in a bar early this morning." It turns out he means three o'clock in the morning. "A couple of men came in and had words with him. One of them pulled out a gun and shot Danny. He died on the way to the hospital. I'm sorry."

Tears run down my mother's cheeks. But she's used to being in charge and dealing with problems. She oversees fifteen stores with a total of two hundred full- and part-time staff. My father always says she's the practical one, the level-headed one. So while the tears are running down her cheeks, she says, "Have you arrested whoever did this?"

"Not yet, Mrs. Carter," Detective Rossetti says.

"But you know who he is," my mother says. "You must, if it happened in a bar."

"We were hoping you might be able to help us with that," Detective Rossetti says.

My mother looks confused again. "I don't understand," she says. "You said he was in a bar."

My father has been out in the front hall the whole time, talking quietly to Detective French. But he hears the change in my mother's voice. He stops talking and comes into the living room.

"Wasn't there anyone else in that bar?" my mother says.

Detective Rossetti glances at Detective French.

"Yes," he says to my mother finally. "Yes, there were other people in the bar. But no one has been able to give us a description yet of the man who shot your son."

"But someone must have seen something," my mother says. "Someone will be able to describe the man who did this."

"We hope so, Mrs. Carter," Detective Rossetti says. "But in the meantime, did Danny say anything to you about any trouble he might have been having with anyone—a friend or an acquaintance?"

My mother shakes her head. "Danny is still in school," she says. "He has a part-time job at a music store. He's doing well. He never said anything to me about any trouble."

I glance at my father, but he refuses to meet my eyes.

"Someone at that bar must have seen something," my mother says again. Then she says, "I don't understand. Why would anyone want to shoot Danny?"

The two detectives tell my parents that they need someone to identify Danny. My father tells them he will do it, but my mother insists on going with him. She gets angry when he tries to get her to stay at home and let him take care of it. She says, "I want to see him. I want to see my baby."

My father asks me if I'll be okay for a little while on my own. I tell him yes. I tell him Caitlin will be coming by soon and maybe she can skip school for a while and stay with me. My father says, "That's a good idea." But after my parents leave and I'm all alone in the house, I don't want anyone there. I don't answer the doorbell when it rings. I don't answer the phone, either. I just sit there in the living room and look at the picture of Danny that's on the mantel, and I think, Boy, now you've gone and done it.

Chapter Three

It's on the news that night—man shot dead in bar. The news story is maybe three sentences long. Danny was shot dead. His death is the twenty-third homicide in the city so far this year. The police are investigating.

My parents don't see the TV news. My mother is upstairs by the time it comes on. She has been up there for hours.

At first, when she and my father got back from identifying Danny's body, she stayed busy by making a list of all the people to call, what to do about the funeral arrangements, what to do about work. But a couple of hours later, she started to cry, and I don't mean just tears. I mean weeping. Sobbing. Moaning. Howling. It got worse and worse. Louder and louder. Finally my father called Shannon's father, who is a doctor, and he prescribed something to calm her down and help make her sleep. By the time the news comes on, my mother has been upstairs in her room for hours, and it's quiet up there.

My father is in the kitchen. He has been calling people—relatives, friends, friends of Danny. He's been saying the same thing over and over again. Danny was shot. No, the police don't know who did it. No, he has no idea why it happened. Yes, he hopes the police will make an arrest soon.

Finally it's too late to call any more people. He comes into the living room where I am, and he says, "You should go to bed."

I want to ask him why he thinks Danny got shot. But I already know the answer to that. I keep thinking about what Detective Rossetti said. There were other people in the bar, but no one has been able to give the police a description of who shot Danny. You don't have to be a genius to figure out what that means. I tell my father I'm not tired. I tell him I'll go to bed soon. He doesn't argue with me.

I stay up most of the night and eventually fall asleep on the couch. I don't wake up until I hear my father open the front door to get the newspaper. When I don't hear the front door close again, I look up over the top of the couch.

My father is standing in the open doorway, reading something on the first page of the newspaper. Then he looks out across the street. He closes the door and goes into the kitchen with the newspaper. When I join him in the kitchen a few minutes later, the newspaper is nowhere in sight. My father is putting a teapot onto a tray along with a mug.

"I'm taking this up to your mother," he says. His face is gray. He looks like he hasn't slept.

After he leaves the kitchen, I look for the newspaper. I find it in the garbage under the sink. I pull it out and see that there is a story about Danny on the front page. In the article, it says that Danny was known to police. It also says that there were over fifty people in the bar at the time Danny was shot. No wonder my father threw the newspaper away.

Scum

The phone rings all morning, and all morning my father answers it. Mostly it's people my parents know who have heard about what happened and who are calling to say how sorry they are. But a few times it's reporters. I hear my father tell them that he has no comment. I hear him say this over and over during one phone call. I hear him say, "Do you have children? Well, imagine that this had just happened to your child. Would you want to talk to a reporter about it?"

But this particular reporter must be good at his job, because a few moments later I hear my father talking about Danny, about how, when he was little, he drew the most amazing pictures, about how he used to talk about going to art school, how he talked about being an architect like my father and how he had finally gone to university to study art history. Then I hear my father say, "He was my son. He was *our* son.

We want to remember him as our son. Do you understand?"

Caitlin comes over later, and my father sends her up to my room to see me. We sit on my bed, and Caitlin tells me how sorry she is about Danny. She asks if the cops have arrested the guy yet. She says she read what it said in the paper. She says with fifty people in that bar, the police will catch the guy for sure. Then she says, "What did they mean when they said Danny was known to the police?"

I tell her I don't know.

That night, when my father is cleaning up the kitchen after a supper that we all barely touched, the phone rings. My father answers it. Mostly he listens. Then he says, "Yes, thank you, I would appreciate that. Thank you."

When he hangs up the phone, he turns to my mother. "That was a reporter I spoke to earlier," he says. "He says the police have found a car that matches the description of a car that was seen driving away from the bar after Danny was…" He shakes his head. "He says the car is parked behind a house in the east end but no one is home. The police have the house under surveillance. He's going to call us as soon as he hears anything."

I feel like I don't breathe for the rest of that night. We all sit in the family room. The TV is on, but the sound is down so low that I can't hear what anyone is saying. But that's okay. I don't really care what's on. My parents don't even look at the TV. We all just sit there, waiting for the phone to ring again, waiting for news.

An hour goes by.

Two hours.

Three hours.

It is close to midnight, and my father says, "We should all try to get some sleep." He stands up.

My mother stays where she is.

My father sits down again.

We wait some more.

The phone rings. My mother's eyes never leave my father as he picks up the phone and says hello. Again he mostly listens. Finally he says, "I see. Well, thank you for calling." He puts down the phone. He looks more tired than I have ever seen him.

"That was that reporter," he says, his voice as lifeless as his face. "It wasn't the right car after all. It was a false alarm."

My mother stands up and goes to him. For the first time since Danny died, she is the strong one. She kneels down in front of my father and puts a hand on his knee. She says to him, "It's okay." And for the first time since

Scum

Danny died—the first time that I know about, anyway—my father cries. The sound is terrible—long, anguished sobs. His shoulders shake. His whole body shakes. My mother wraps her arms around him and holds him and says over and over, "It's okay."

Chapter Four

Danny's funeral is held on Monday morning at a funeral home instead of at our church. The service is led by someone I've never seen before instead of by our church minister. When I ask my father why, he says, "It's what your mother wanted." The guy who does the service calls me Margaret instead of Megan. He says things about Danny that

Scum

I haven't heard anyone say since I was a little kid, like how Danny loved dogs and how he liked to ski. The last time Danny talked about getting a dog was when he was twelve years old. The last time he went skiing was when he was in high school. This guy doesn't know what he's talking about. I glance at my mother to see how she's reacting, but her face is like a mask. I can't tell what she's thinking.

After the service, we all go to another room in the funeral home, where there are tables and chairs set up and sandwiches and cakes for people to eat. My mother and father move from table to table to thank everyone for coming. Everyone says the same thing: "I'm so sorry." No one asks any questions about what happened. As far as I can tell, nobody even says anything privately about it. No one wants to hurt my parents.

After the funeral, we go home—my mother and my father and I. One of my mother's friends offers to come over, but my mother tells her, no, it's okay, she's tired and she wants to try to get some sleep. But when we get home, my mother doesn't go up to her room to lie down. Instead she goes down to the basement. My father goes down maybe two hours later, when she still hasn't come up again.

"What's she doing?" I ask him when he comes back upstairs.

"Looking at things," my father says. He doesn't say what things. He doesn't have to. I know. When Danny moved out, he left behind everything but his clothes and his music. He even left most of his sketchbooks and art supplies at home. My mother packed everything into boxes and put it downstairs. She changed his room into an upstairs den. She is down in the basement, going through Danny's things. She doesn't come up for hours.

I go back to school the day after the funeral. I feel like everyone knows what happened to Danny. I walk down the hall and kids turn to look at me, even kids I barely know, kids in lower grades than me, kids who aren't in any of my classes, kids who are new to my school, kids who never even met Danny. They all turn to look at me. Now I am the girl whose brother was shot dead in a bar. I hear them talking in low voices. I can guess what they're saying about Danny and about my family. I act like I don't care. What else can I do?

My mother doesn't go back to work. She doesn't even get out of bed. My dad stays home too. He keeps making her cups of tea and mugs of soup. He makes her toast. He makes sandwiches.

He takes these things up to her on a tray and eventually carries them back down again untouched. I hear him talking to her sometimes. I hear him say the word doctor. He says Shannon's father's name. My mother stays in bed for days, but Shannon's father never appears.

My father looks at the newspaper every day, but there is nothing about Danny. He is never mentioned on the TV news either. It's as if it never happened.

Every day my dad calls Detective Rossetti. Every day he asks Detective Rossetti if there's been any progress. Every day he gets the same answer: there is nothing new to report. Then one day I am in the kitchen making myself a cup of tea, and I see Detective Rossetti's business card stuck to the fridge door. My father isn't home. He has finally gone back to work. My mother is upstairs in bed. The bed is piled high with photograph albums and school yearbooks and drawings and paintings and sketchbooks from when Danny was serious about wanting to be an artist. My mother looks at them when she is awake. Right now it's quiet up there.

I look at Detective Rossetti's business card. I pick up the phone and punch in his number. I carry the phone with me into the family room at the back of the house so that if my mother is awake upstairs, she won't be able to hear me. To my surprise, Detective Rossetti answers, his tone brisk, efficient: "Detective Rossetti, Homicide."

When I tell him who I am, his voice changes. He asks me how I am. He asks about my parents too. I ask him why no one in the bar saw anything.

"It was a rough crowd in there," he says. "You know what I mean, Megan?" Then he tells me what he usually tells my father—he says he's sorry, but there has been no progress in the case.

On a Wednesday night nearly two weeks after Danny was shot, I hear my father leave the spare bedroom, where he has been sleeping since the funeral, and go downstairs. I get up and go downstairs after him. I find him in the front hall, pulling on a jacket and fishing his car keys out of the brass bowl on the front hall table.

"Where are you going?" I say.

"Out," he says, sounding in that instant just like Danny used to sound, when he still lived at home and when he used to leave the house when everyone else was getting ready to go to bed.

"Out where?" I say.

He doesn't answer my question. Instead he says, "Stay here. Keep your mother company."

My mother has barely said a word to me since it happened. If I go into her room, she doesn't always look at me.

When she does, she looks right through me, as though I'm a window and if she looks hard enough, she can see Danny through me.

"She doesn't want company," I say. That's why my father is sleeping in the spare room now. "Where are you going?" I say again.

"Downtown."

"Downtown where? It's late."

He finally tells me.

I understand what he is doing. He thinks that if he can find out who killed Danny, my mother will get out of bed again. She will eat again. She may even smile again, although I don't think he expects that to happen any time soon.

I think about what Detective Rossetti said, but that only helps me make up my mind.

"I'm going with you," I say. "And you can't stop me."

He doesn't even try. If you ask me, he wants me to go with him. Unlike my mother, he wants company.

Chapter Five

I have never before driven downtown so late on a weeknight. There are bright lights everywhere, even in the office towers, even though they are empty except for the cleaning staff. But the streets are much quieter than they are during the day, and my father has no trouble finding a place to park. We get out of the car. My father draws in a deep breath before he starts across the street. I have to scramble to catch up to him.

I've never been in the bar where my brother was killed, and I almost don't get in now. A heavyset man is standing just inside the door. He stops us and demands to know how old I am. He demands to see ID.

"Please," my father says. "The boy who was shot here—he was my son. He was her brother."

The heavyset man looks at me. There is no sympathy in his small eyes. No pity. No emotion at all.

"Were you here that night?" my father asks him.

"I didn't see nothing," the man says right away, without my father having to ask him.

I think about my English teacher, who is crazy about grammar, and what he would say if he were here: *If you didn't see nothing, then you must have seen something.* But even if that's what the heavyset man means, I don't think he'll tell my father. His eyes are too small, too cold, too uncaring.

My father looks into the man's eyes. I can see he is disappointed. He tries to move past the man, but the man steps in front of my father again.

"She can't go in there," he says. "She's too young."

My father looks back over his shoulder at the street and at our car, which is parked on the other side. It's late and the street is empty.

"I can't leave her outside," my father says. "It's not safe."

The heavyset man crosses his arms over his chest. He is settling in now, a permanent roadblock.

"Please," my father says. "We just want to go inside for a few minutes. We just want to talk to some people."

I peek past the man into the gloomy interior of the bar. I see a cavernous room. There is a bar along one side. A man stands behind it, pouring drinks and putting them on a tray for a server, a young woman in tight pants and a tight T-shirt. I look at the rest of the room. At first I have trouble seeing if there is anyone else in there, it's that dark. Then I begin to make out shapes—people huddled around tables. Men, mostly, but with a scattering of women. I wonder if Danny was a regular in this dismal place. I wonder if he came here for business or for pleasure.

The bartender looks over at me. He sets one last drink onto the server's tray. As the server walks away from the bar, the bartender comes toward us. He is almost as tall as the bouncer. He is wearing black jeans and a black T-shirt. A giant snake tattoo coils around his left arm all the way from his wrist and disappears under the sleeve of his T-shirt. He glances at my father and me. Then he says to the bouncer, "Problem?"

"They want to come in," the bouncer says. "She's underage."

The bartender looks at my father and shakes his head.

"I let a kid in here who's underage, I can lose my licence," he says to my father. He sounds more reasonable than the bouncer.

"You're the owner?" my father says.

The bartender nods.

My father looks relieved. Finally, someone he can talk to, someone who will understand.

"The young man who was killed here, that was my son," my father says.

The bartender looks surprised. My father is tall, but he's thin and balding. He wears glasses. He doesn't look anything like Danny, who is…was…strong and tough and confident—overconfident.

He doesn't look anything like the father of a guy who would get himself shot in a bar at three in the morning.

"I just want to talk to your customers," my father says. "Please. My wife won't even get out of bed. I just want to talk to your customers and see if anyone can help us."

I can't tell what the bartender is thinking. I can't tell if he feels sorry for my father or if he thinks my father is pathetic. But he finally nods. The bouncer steps aside. As I start to follow my father into the gloomy cavern, the bartender says, "I don't think anybody saw anything." My father turns to him, and the bartender says, "I was here myself that night, and I didn't see anything."

I look at the bartender's face. I peer into his eyes. I am sure he's lying to my father. I'm also sure he knows what I'm thinking but he doesn't care.

Scum

I follow my father around the place. He is polite to everyone. At every table he approaches, he begins by saying, "I'm sorry to disturb you." Then he introduces himself. If he notices that nobody seems to care who he is, he doesn't let it show. He asks everyone at every table if they were in the bar when Danny was shot. Everybody says the same thing: No. Not only did nobody see anything, but nobody was there. Some of them barely glance at my father. Some of them don't look at him at all. They are all rough people. They're not like the people who live in my neighborhood.

Again I wonder what Danny was doing in this place and how often he came here. No one expresses any sympathy for my father. But my father doesn't stop until he has spoken to every single person at every single table.

When he has finished, he goes to the bar, where there are several men sitting on stools, drinking in silence. A couple of them watch the TV, which has the sound turned down low. I hang back. The truth: I am embarrassed for my father. He is talking so politely to everyone. He is practically begging for their help. But no one will help him.

The bartender listens to my father ask his questions. I see him shake his head. He knows my father will get nowhere. He knew it when he let my father into the bar.

I step forward now. I think if I stay close to my father, I can protect him somehow. I can stop him from noticing how everyone in the bar sees him.

That's when I notice that there is someone besides the bartender behind the bar. A kid. He doesn't look much older than me. He is wearing an apron, and he is stacking dirty glasses and plates in a big plastic tub. He glances at me as he hoists the tub and starts to carry it toward the back of the huge room. He glances at me, and I see something in his eyes that I haven't seen in any other eyes in this place.

I tug my father's arm. I point at the kid.

Chapter Six

My father calls out, "Excuse me." He starts to move toward the kid, who is still walking toward the back of the bar. At first I think that he hasn't heard my father. Then I realize: He doesn't know that my father's polite *excuse me* is directed at him.

The bartender comes out from behind the bar and grabs my father's arm, forcing him to a halt.

"But I just want to ask—" my father begins.

"He wasn't here that night," the bartender says.

The kid glances back over his shoulder, and I see something else in his eyes. He starts to shake his head.

"You've got a job to do," the bartender says sharply to the kid. "Or maybe you don't need a job anymore."

The kid hurries to the kitchen, carrying the tub full of dirty glasses and plates.

"He wasn't here that night," the bartender says again. "You've talked to everyone. You should go home."

My father looks around the gloomy bar. A few people look back at him. He says, "Come on, Meggie. It's late, and you have school tomorrow."

We drive home in silence. Later, when I am in bed, I hear my father in the spare room beside my room. He is weeping.

Another week goes by. Now it is three weeks since Danny died. I come home from school to a big surprise. For once, my mother isn't in her room. She's in the kitchen. She is cooking. She doesn't exactly smile at me, but she does look at me. She says, "I called work today. I'm going back on Monday."

I say the only thing I can think of: "That's great, Mom."

My father gets home at his regular time. I am on my way upstairs when he comes through the front door. He pauses and sniffs the air. He looks at me, a puzzled expression on his face.

"Are you making supper tonight?" he says. "It smells good."

"It's Mom," I say. "She's cooking. She's in the kitchen."

My father looks surprised. He smiles. I realize it's the first time I've seen him smile since the police came to the door three weeks ago.

Scum

My mother calls me to set the table. My father follows me through to the kitchen. He kisses my mother on the cheek. She doesn't exactly smile at him, but she doesn't pull away either. She says, "Supper is almost ready."

"I have to make a call," my father says. He picks up the phone and carries it through to the family room. I know who he's calling. He calls the same person every night—Detective Rossetti. I hear him apologize for phoning again. I imagine Detective Rossetti's voice the way it was that time I called.

My mother looks through to the family room. She watches my father as he listens to whatever Detective Rossetti is saying. She hears him say, "Well, thank you for your time."

When he carries the phone back into the kitchen, she says, "Who was that?"

"That detective," my father says.

A shadow crosses my mother's face.

"And?" she says.

My father sighs. "And nothing," he says. "There's still been no progress."

I am afraid my mother will fall apart. I am afraid she will start to cry again. I am afraid she will go back upstairs to her room. But she doesn't do any of these things. Instead she nods, and she says, "Dinner is on the table."

When I wake up on Monday morning, it's like everything has gone back to the way it used to be. My mother is dressed in a business suit and is bustling out the door with her briefcase when I come down the stairs. She tosses a goodbye over her shoulder at me.

My father is stuffing papers into his briefcase when I go into the kitchen. Without looking up from what he is doing, he tells me he has an important meeting this afternoon and that he will be home late. He also tells me that my mother has a lot of catching up to do and that she will probably be late too. He asks me if I'll be okay on my own.

When I don't answer right away, he pauses to look at me. "Meggie?" he says. "You'll be okay, right?"

I tell him, "Sure." I even smile at him when he kisses me on the cheek before dashing out the door.

When he is gone, I think, Did the last three weeks happen or did I dream them? I think, How can a person die, and three weeks later, everything seems like it's back to normal? It takes me most of the day before I realize that I am wrong. Nothing is back to normal.

That afternoon, English class. We're reading a play. Shakespeare. *Hamlet*. And Hamlet, the lead guy, is talking to a gravedigger.

Which makes me, just like that, think about Danny's funeral and the guy who called me Margaret instead of Megan, and no one corrected him. Then he said all those things about Danny that maybe once upon a time were true, but they weren't true recently. And the next thing you know, I'm crying.

Caitlin notices it first. She sits right beside me. Then, I can't help it, I sniffle, and another girl looks at me. Then that girl pokes the girl in front of her, and she turns around. Pretty soon there are enough people looking at me that it makes the teacher stop what she's saying. She peers at me. She says, "Megan, are you all right?"

I start to nod because that's what you're supposed to do, right? You're supposed to say, yeah, you're fine. But I don't feel fine. I feel sad. So I stop nodding, and I shake my head instead. I can't stand all those people looking at me. I can't stand what they're probably thinking. Poor Megan, did you hear what happened to her brother? Do you know what her brother was into? And that's it. I get up and I run out of the classroom. I don't stop running until I am down the stairs and out of the school, even though Mr. Tesco sees me fly past and he calls my name. I don't care.

I run and I run until I am up at the highway. Cars are rushing by me, and I think how easy it would be to dance into the path of one. Then I think about my father and how sad he has been and the phone calls he makes every day. I think about who he will talk to if anything happens to me. I think about whether he would be able to stop himself from telling my mother everything. Then I see a bus in the distance. It's coming toward me. I fumble in my backpack for my wallet, and I count out exact change. When the bus pulls over to where I am standing, I get on.

An hour later, I am standing across the street from the bar where my brother died. It's daytime, and I can see now how rundown the place is, what a dive it is. I try to picture Danny in a place like that at three in the morning. I try to picture what he was doing in there. I try to picture someone walking up to him and saying something to him—probably something angry—and then shooting him.

Then I think of it another way. I think of someone walking up to Danny and maybe asking him something, and Danny doing what he does best, giving the guy some smartass answer, making some sarcastic response. It wouldn't surprise me. Danny thinks…thought…he was smarter than anyone else. Danny had an answer for everything, and if it was an answer that could get him a laugh, even better. I picture Danny being a smartass, only he's picked the wrong guy or the wrong day, and the next thing you know, someone is calling 911.

I'm standing there, thinking all of this, when I see someone come around the corner and walk to the front door of the bar. I see his hand reach out to open the door. I see that hand pause, and the person who is about to go into the bar turns and looks at me instead. Then he comes across the street toward me.

Chapter Seven

It's the same kid who was carrying the tub of dirty glasses and plates the night my father and I went to the bar so that my father could talk to the customers. Now that he's up close to me, I see that he is scrawny, with eyes that look too big for his face, and soft lips like a girl's. His hair is long and wavy. He keeps raking it out of his eyes with one hand. He says, "Hey."

"Hey," I say.

"You're the girl who was here last week," he says. "With that man."

"That was my dad," I say.

The kid looks around. "You here alone now?"

I nod.

"You're not going back in there, are you?" he says, frowning.

"My brother was killed in there," I say.

There is a long pause before he says, "I heard about that."

"The cops say there were a lot of people in the bar when he was killed. But they say they haven't been able to find out anything. They haven't even been able to get a description of the guy who did it."

"Well, it's pretty dark in there," the kid says. "And the people who go in there, they're the kind of people who mind their own business."

"You work there, right?" I say. He nods. "Did you know my brother?"

"I know who he is," he says. "I've seen him around." He looks me over and shakes his head. "It's hard to believe he was your brother."

"Why do you say that?"

"You know," he says with a shrug.

I tell him I don't know. I tell him I have no idea what he's talking about. His cheeks turn pink.

"I mean, you seem so nice," he says. "Your dad too, the way he went around talking to everyone, saying please and thank you. He seems real nice."

"So what are you saying?" I ask. "Are you saying that Danny wasn't nice?" I know Danny. I know how he could be. But it's one thing for me to think he could be a real jerk sometimes. It's one thing for me to even say it out loud. But for someone else to think that about Danny, about *my* brother, especially now that he's dead—that's another thing altogether.

"He was my brother," I tell this kid. "He used to take care of me. He used to walk me to school. He used to buy me ice cream out of the money he made delivering flyers around the neighborhood." And it's all true, which I guess is why I start crying again.

"I'm sorry," the kid says. "I don't have any brothers or sisters. I'm sorry. I didn't mean anything."

"There were so many people in there the night he died," I say bitterly. "And you expect me to believe that not a single one of them saw anything? What kind of people drink in that bar, anyway? What kind of people can see someone get shot right in front of them and not want to tell the police what happened? What if one of their kids got shot? How would they feel if *I* saw something like that, and I just kept my mouth shut?"

I'm shouting at the kid now, and he starts to look nervous. He glances back across the street. Just as he does, the front door of the bar opens, and the bartender steps out. He looks over at us. Then he yells, "Titch! Get in here!"

Titch? I look at the kid. What kind of name is Titch?

The kid looks uncomfortable. "I gotta go," he says. He hesitates. "Look, I'm sorry about your brother. People are complicated, you know. Sometimes you see one side of them, sometimes you see another side. I didn't really know your brother. I didn't really get to see all the different sides of him."

"Titch!" the bartender roars. "*Now!*"

Titch dashes back across the street. When he gets there, the bartender cuffs him on the back of the head and shoves him through the door into the bar. He glances around, like he's checking to see if anyone else is watching. Then he scowls at me across the street before disappearing inside.

The house is empty when I get home, even though it's way past suppertime. There are two messages for me on the phone—one from my mother and one from my father. They both tell me the same thing. They both say they are going to be late and that I should fix myself something to eat. But I'm not hungry.

I'm lying on the sofa in the family room. The TV is on, but I'm not really watching it. Mostly I have it on for the sound, so that there's something filling up the house besides my heart beating and me breathing.

My mother comes home first. I hear her drop her briefcase in the front hall. She comes through to the kitchen and stands at the counter for a moment, looking over at me.

"Did you get something to eat?" she says.

"I made myself a sandwich," I say. A lie.

She nods and turns around to leave the kitchen. Just then my father appears. He looks like he's going to say something, but my mother walks past him without a word. I hear her footsteps as she goes upstairs. I hear the door to her bedroom click shut.

My father watches her. After she has gone, he looks at the spot where she used to be. It takes a few moments before he turns to me.

"Did you get something to eat?" he says.

"I had a sandwich," I say.

He nods and starts to turn away.

"Dad?"

He turns again.

"Did you call Detective Rossetti today?" I say.

He nods again. "He tells me they haven't given up," he says. "But they've hit a roadblock, Meggie. They have nothing to go on. He says the case will stay open and active. But you know what it's like in the city. There's always someone else getting killed. Those detectives work hard. They put in long hours."

In other words, my father has given up.

"Did you have supper, Dad?" I say. "You want me to make you something?"

"I ate before I came home," he says. I notice how his suit hangs on him like it's three sizes too big. I know he is lying to me. But sometimes you don't feel like eating. Sometimes you just don't care.

Chapter Eight

Three nights later, the phone rings and I answer it.

"Is this Megan Carter?" a voice says.

"Yes."

"This is Titch. You know, from the bar?"

I am so surprised that I almost drop the phone. "How did you get my phone number?" I say.

"I saw the notice in the newspaper after it happened." He sounds as surprised by my question as I am by his voice. "It had your name and your parents' names. I looked you up."

Oh.

For a moment there is silence between us. He is the first to speak again.

"I just wanted to see how you were," he says. "You know, because you were so upset the last time I saw you."

I've been thinking about what I said to him. I've been thinking that maybe it's dishonest of me to act like Danny was some kind of angel when I know he wasn't. My father and I both know. But when Titch hinted at the same thing, I got mad at him and told him he didn't know what he was talking about.

"I'm sorry," I say. "I shouldn't have yelled at you like that."

"Yeah, well, I'm sorry too," he says. "He was your brother. And you're not supposed to say bad things about people who have just…" His voice trails off, and I wonder if he's afraid to use certain words, like *died* or *dead*. I wonder if he thinks those words will make me cry.

"It's okay," I say. "It was nice of you to come over and talk to me."

"You seem like a nice person," he says. He has a soft voice and a quiet way of speaking, and suddenly I don't want him to hang up. So I say, "Have you been working at that bar for a long time?"

"About a year," he says. "Dave, the guy who owns the place, he kind of looks out for me."

"Looks out for you?" I wonder what he means.

"He used to go with my mom. When she died, he let me crash at his place. He's always after me all the time to get my homework done. He gave me a job too. He's a good guy."

"So you're around that bar a lot," I say.

"Yeah."

"And you know a lot of the regulars," I say.

"Yeah," he says again, only now I hear caution in his voice, like he's afraid of what I might say next.

So I don't ask him any more about the bar. Instead I tell him how weird it is around the house. I tell him how my mother used to bustle around here, talking about work, trying to get a meal on the table, how she used to boast all the time that she was the queen of multitasking, but now she's quiet all the time, and when she's at home, she's up in her room alone. I tell him about how sad my father is, maybe even sadder than my mother because, after all, Danny was his son, and aren't men supposed to have a special bond with their sons? I tell him about the funeral, and how

I can't figure out why my mother wanted to have it at the funeral home instead of at the church, and why she didn't ask our minister to give the service but instead had some stranger do it who didn't get my name right and talked about what Danny was like years ago instead of what he was like now.

There was silence again when I said that. Then Titch said, "Maybe that's what she wanted to remember most—what he was like when he was a little boy."

I think about that. It makes perfect sense.

"I like dogs too," Titch says.

"Do you have one? What kind?"

"I had one for a while. Just a mutt, but a nice dog, you know? Smart."

"What happened to him?"

"He got hit by a car. I saw it happen. The car that hit him didn't even stop."

"Did you report it to the police?" I say.

"Naw. The cops don't care about a dog, especially a mutt. But I'm saving up. As soon as I get enough money together, I'm going to get a purebred. A chocolate Lab."

"That's a big dog," I say.

"That's what I want. A big dog."

We talk a little longer. Then I hear someone call his name.

"Are you at work?" I say.

"I'm on my break." I hear his name being called again, and I picture that bartender with his angry face. "I gotta go," Titch says.

I think about him all night. I think how he's been working at that bar for about a year now. I think how he must know a lot of the regulars. I think how it might be different if Titch were to ask around. People who know him might tell him things that they would never tell my father, maybe even things that they would never tell the police. I can't stop thinking about it.

Chapter Nine

I don't pay attention in school the next day. Most of my teachers don't bother me. Most of them are afraid to push me or yell at me. Most of them think I will burst into tears if they say anything to me. So I keep my head down, and I think about Titch. I can't wait until the last bell of the day rings. As soon as it does, I head up to the highway and stand there impatiently waiting for the bus.

When I get to the bar, I don't hesitate for one second. I walk right into the place like I own it. There is no bouncer at the door. I guess it's too early for him. The place isn't crowded, but there are people at a lot of the tables and in a lot of the booths. A few of them glance up. Most of them don't pay any attention.

A door opens at the back of the bar. Titch comes through carrying a massive tray that is filled with clean glasses. It's so big that he staggers a little under its weight. A look of surprise crosses his face when he spots me, and the tray wobbles. For one terrible moment, I think it is going to tip and all the glasses are going to crash to the floor. But Titch bites his lower lip and concentrates on what he is doing. He gets to the bar and puts the tray down. Then he comes over to me and says in a low voice, "What are you doing here?"

Scum

"I want to talk to you," I say.

The door at the back of the bar opens again and someone else walks through. It's the bartender. Titch grabs my arm when he sees him. He grabs it so hard that I say, "Ow!" That's when the bartender notices who is with Titch. He starts toward us. He does not look happy to see me. Titch glances at him, and his face changes.

"What do you want?" he says angrily, his voice much louder now, like I am the last person he wants to see.

"Yeah," the bartender says. He is right beside Titch now. "What *do* you want? You shouldn't even be in here. You're too young."

I decide to ignore the bartender. I focus on Titch.

"I need to talk to you," I say.

"I'm busy," Titch says. "I've got work to do." His voice is cold and hard. He doesn't sound like the same person

I spoke to on the phone last night. He doesn't look like the same person who talked to me out on the street a few days ago.

"Are you going to be a good girl and get out of here?" the bartender says. "Or do I have to escort you out?"

When I don't move, he grabs me by the elbow and pulls me toward the door. I dig in my heels and look at Titch for help. The bartender's long fingers bite into my arm. I am going to have finger-shaped bruises all around my elbow. I try to resist, but the bartender is tall and strong. He drags me toward the door, and there is nothing I can do to stop him. I look at Titch. He looks back at me, but I don't see anything nice in his face now. The bartender opens the front door and pushes me through onto the sidewalk.

"You come in here again, and I'll have to call the police," he says.

"You're not allowed in here. You understand me?"

I tell myself that there is no way I am going to give this guy the satisfaction of seeing me cry. I try to shake him off me. But he holds tight.

"The police have already been here," he says. "They already talked to people. Nobody saw what happened. But I'll tell you something, little girl. Your brother was no angel. He was a real piece of work. If you don't believe me, you can ask around. You'll find out the same thing. The cops already know it. They know your brother. You hear what I'm telling you? So stop coming around here. It's not going to do anyone any good. And leave Titch alone. He didn't see what happened. He didn't see anything."

When he finally lets go of me, he gives me a little shove, and I almost fall over. He goes back into the bar.

I stand on the sidewalk for a few minutes, rubbing my elbow where he was holding me. I stand there, and I realize that I am hoping Titch will come out. I am hoping he'll come to see if I am okay. I'm hoping that I can talk to him and that he will help me. But then I remember the look on his face and how cold his voice was. And there I am again, doing what I said I wasn't going to do. There I am crying.

I find my way back to the bus stop.

I look out the window all the way home. Sometimes I focus on the window itself. I see the shadow of my face in it, like a ghost's face, because through it I can see houses and trees and cars and utility poles zipping by. Sometimes I focus on my face instead. When I do, I see tears dribbling down my cheeks.

It's quiet in the house when I get home. My mother's bedroom door is shut, which means that she is in there, maybe sleeping, maybe looking at pictures of Danny. The door to the spare room is shut too. But it opens as I go by, and my father looks out.

"Where have you been?" he says.

"At the library," I say. "I got behind in my work. I'm trying to catch up."

"It's hard times now," my father says. "But it'll get better. After a while, it'll feel different." He says it, but something in his face tells me he doesn't really believe it.

It's late when the phone rings. My father answers it. He raps gently on my door.

"It's for you," he says. "It's a boy."

I take the phone from him and say hello.

"It's me," a voice says. "It's Titch."

I put my hand over the mouthpiece and tell my father it's a boy from my history class. I tell him we're doing group projects. Then I take the phone into my room and close the door.

"Look, I'm sorry," Titch says. "But you shouldn't have come down there. You—"

I press the button to end the call.

The phone rings again a few seconds later.

I say hello. It's Titch again. I hang up again. Right after I do, I press the ON button. Now anyone who calls will end up in voice mail. I leave the phone that way all night. In the morning, I check it. There are no messages. I tell myself I don't care. I tell myself I hate Titch. I tell myself I wish he had a brother and I wish his brother would get shot. Then he would know what it's like.

Chapter Ten

I am angry all the way to school. I am angry at my locker. I am angry when Caitlin asks me if I want to go to the mall with her and Shannon. Right. Like I care about the mall. I slam my locker and walk away from her. I hear her behind me saying, "What did I do? What did I say?" But I don't turn around because I am so angry.

I am angry because of what Titch did when I went to the bar.

I am angry because he called me.

I am angry because of the look on his face the first time I saw him.

I am angry because of the look on his face yesterday.

I am angry at everything he's said to me and at everything he hasn't said.

But mostly I am angry about what the bartender said when he pushed me out of the bar. He told my father that Titch wasn't at the bar when Danny was shot. But that's not what he told me. He told me, "He didn't see what happened. He didn't see anything."

He didn't see anything.

So at lunchtime, I ditch the rest of my classes and head downtown. I don't go directly to the bar. Instead I think about the direction Titch had been coming from when I came down here alone the first time. I remember what he said about the bartender making sure he did his schoolwork. I decide that Titch must have been coming to the bar from school. So I wait a couple of blocks from the bar in a little park that's wedged between a couple of tall buildings. I wait and I wait, and finally I see Titch. He's got a backpack over one shoulder, and he's striding along with a serious expression on his face. I step out in front of him and enjoy the look of surprise on his face. Then I am confused, because his face isn't hard now and his voice isn't cold.

"Megan," he says. "I kept calling you last night, but all I got was voice mail."

"I left the phone off the hook," I say.

"I guess you're mad at me, huh?" he says.

"The first time you called me, you were nice," I say. "I thought you were okay."

His face reminds me of a puppy's that's hoping for a treat but is also maybe afraid you'll find out it peed on your mom's new carpet or chewed her favorite shoes. I look him right in the eyes, and I say, "You were there that night, weren't you? You were in the bar the night Danny was shot."

His eyes skip away from mine. His cheeks start to turn pink. He turns his head away, and he says, "No."

"Yes, you were," I say. "That's why you can't look at me now. You're a nice guy and you know this is important to me. That's why you called me—because you know how I feel. Because even if you don't have a brother, you can imagine what it's like to lose somebody you care about. You're a nice guy, and you're ashamed because you were in the bar and you saw something. You saw something or you know something, but you haven't told the police.

Scum

I think you're protecting whoever killed my brother."

He looks at me. He's shaking his head, but I know I'm right.

"I know you're not the only person who saw something," I tell him. "I've been in there. Twice. I know you can't have fifty people in there and not a single one of them sees anything when someone gets shot. I'm not stupid, Titch. I know it's impossible."

He's still shaking his head, but slowly. He holds his head up and looks right at me. He says, "I'm not protecting anybody. I didn't see anything."

My heart feels like it's going to shatter into hundreds of jagged little pieces, and each piece is going to cut into me. Titch is lying. He's standing right in front of me and he's lying to me.

But that isn't what makes my heart feel like it's going to explode. No. The thing that does that is that I know I am right about him. He's lying, and he's ashamed of himself for doing it. So I try again.

I say, "He was my brother. He was part of my life since the day I was born. I loved him. My parents loved him. It's bad enough he died, but someone murdered him. It's killing my parents that whoever did this is still walking around free. It's not right, Titch. You have to tell me what you know. You have to tell the police."

He looks away from me again. He's chewing the inside of his lip, which tells me that he's thinking.

"Please, Titch."

Cars have been passing us on the street the whole time we've been talking. A car passes us now. It slows down. The driver turns his head to look at us. I recognize him. It's the bouncer from the bar. He looks directly at Titch. Then he looks at me.

"I have to go," Titch says. "I'm gonna be late. Dave gets mad when I'm late." He starts to walk away from me, but I grab his arm and pull him back.

"I know you know something," I say. "I know you saw something. I can go to the police. I can tell them you're hiding something."

His face turns red. He gets mad. He says, "Go to the police if you want. Tell them whatever you want. I don't care. It's not going to change anything. I'm not going to say anything to them."

I stare at him. I don't want to be right, but I know I am because now he isn't saying that he didn't see anything. No, now he is saying that he isn't going to say anything.

I hear a car door slam. The bouncer has parked across the street. He's getting out of his car, and he's looking at Titch and me.

"Please," I say to Titch. I'm still holding on to his arm so he won't walk away from me.

He shakes me off. His face is up close to mine when he says, "You tell the police whatever you want. I don't care. *They* don't even care. Your brother was dealing drugs. Everyone knew it. The cops knew it. It's why they don't care. It's why no one cares. It's just one less drug dealer on the street."

He walks away from me, and this time I let him go. I watch the bouncer go after him. I stand there for a few moments, tears stinging my eyes. I don't know who I hate more: Titch or Danny.

Chapter Eleven

I can tell something is wrong the minute I walk through the door. My mother's voice reaches me from the family room. She says, "No." Her voice is loud and sharp.

Then I hear my father's voice, softer than hers. He's trying to convince her of something.

"It might work," he says. "I talked to that detective. He said it might work."

What might work? I wonder.

"No," my mother says again.

"But I already set it up," my father says. "They're going to hold a press conference. They're going to announce it."

"Tell them you changed your mind," my mother says.

"No," my father says. For the first time since Danny died, his voice sounds as sharp as my mother's. "I'm going to do it. If there's even the smallest chance that this could help the police catch whoever killed Danny, I'm going to do it."

While I listen to him, I walk through to the family room.

"Do what?" I say.

My mother whirls around to face me. "Your father and I are having a private conversation," she says. "Go to your room."

I ignore her.

"Do what?" I say to my father.

"Offer a reward," he says. "For information leading to the arrest of whoever killed Danny. That detective says that it might work." He glances at my mother. "They're going to announce it tonight."

"Either you call them and tell them that you've changed your mind or I will," my mother says.

"You'll do no such thing," my father says. "What's the matter with you? Don't you want them to catch the guy?"

My mother turns to me. "Go to your room," she says.

I don't move. I can't believe what I'm hearing.

"Dad's right," I say. "If it will help the police find out who did it, then it's the right thing to do."

My mother goes into the kitchen. She grabs Detective Rossetti's business card, which is attached to the fridge with a magnet. Then she picks up the phone and starts punching in a phone number—Detective Rossetti's phone number.

"What are you doing?" I say.

My father crosses the family room in a flash. He grabs the phone out of her hand.

"Give that back to me," my mother says. She tries to snatch the phone from him, but he holds it out of her reach.

"Fine," she says. She marches into the front hall. Her purse is on the floor next to her briefcase. She picks it up and fishes out her cell phone. She flips it open and starts punching in Detective Rossetti's phone number again.

I glance at my father. His face is red. He lunges at my mother and tries to pry the cell phone from her hand. I have never seen my father do anything like that. My mother yells at him. My father makes another grab for her cell phone. She slaps him across the face.

Scum

For a moment nobody moves. My father looks as stunned as I am. Then he slaps her back. My mother's cell phone clatters to the floor. It is a moment before she stoops down to pick it up. But before her hand reaches it, my father kicks it out of the way.

"You are *not* calling that detective," he says in a hard voice. "Maybe you don't care that Danny's killer is walking around out there, but I do. I'm going to do whatever it takes to find that person and make sure he gets what he deserves."

My mother is very still. She doesn't try to pick up her phone. She says, "Arthur came into my office today." Arthur is my mother's boss. "Do you know what he asked me?"

My father doesn't say anything.

"He asked me if the police were any closer to finding out who killed Danny."

My father still doesn't say anything.

"And then he told me that he'd read an article in the paper right after Danny died. He said that it said in the article that Danny was known to the police. He stood right there in my office and he asked me, what does that mean, Maria? What does it mean, he was known to the police?"

I can tell that my father is holding his breath now. He glances at me. He wants me to keep my mouth shut. Even now, after the way my mother has treated him, he wants to protect her.

"Maria…" he begins.

I look down at the floor. I was the first one to know about Danny. I found out because one time when he came over he asked me if my friends and I ever partied. He was in a good mood that day. He asked me to tell my friends, if they ever needed anything to put them in a party mood, he could hook them up. I laughed. I thought he was kidding.

Scum

He wasn't.

I told him it was stupid. I told him he could get busted. He told me I was the stupid one.

"Everyone does it," he said. "And the money?" He grinned at me. "The money's good, Meggie."

My father found out because the hospital called him. Danny had been beaten up. He didn't want to say what happened or who did it, but he was hurt badly and he didn't know what else to do, so he got them to call my father, and my father and I went to the hospital to see him. The police were there, but Danny didn't want to talk to them. He didn't want to tell them anything. My father didn't understand. He talked to one of the cops, who told him what they suspected.

When my father confronted Danny, Danny just laughed. He laughed even though he was all beat up. He said, "They got nothing on me."

My father waited until the doctor was finished with Danny. Then we drove Danny home. When we got to Danny's place, my father and Danny had a big argument. Danny wouldn't listen. He said it was his life. He said he knew what he was doing. He said, "Everybody does it. If there was no market, I'd be out of business like that. But there is a market. It's just a product. I'm just a businessman. I'm a smart one too."

My father looked at all the cuts and bruises on Danny. He looked at how he could hardly breathe because it hurt so much. He said, "Yeah, I can see that." Then he told Danny to stay away from the house until he was better. He said, "If your mother saw you like this, it would break her heart." On the way home, he said to me, "Don't breathe a word of this to your mother. It would kill her."

And now here we are.

Chapter Twelve

"Maria," my father says. "There's something—"

"No," my mother says. She shakes her head. "I don't want to talk about it. I want you to call that police detective. Tell him you've changed your mind. I want you to tell him there's no reward. Please, Paul? Please, just do it, and I swear I won't ask you for another thing, ever."

"He was my son," my father says.

"He's gone," my mother says. "No matter what the police do, that's never going to change."

"But—"

"Say you announce a reward," my mother says slowly. "And say that because of that, because someone thinks he can make money from it, someone tells the police something. Say someone tells the police exactly who did it. What do you think will happen then?"

"The police will arrest the guy," my father says. "Isn't that what you want?"

"And then what?" my mother says. "You think this person is going to admit that he did it?" She shakes her head. "Of course not," she says. "He'll get a lawyer and there will be a trial. And what do you think his lawyer is going to do?" She looks at my father. "What do you think he's going to say about Danny? He's going to say that Danny was known to the police. He might even get some police officers to testify and to say what they knew about Danny. They'll explain what it means when someone is known to the police. It will be in the papers, Paul. It will be on the news. Right now, people are whispering. I know they are. But that's all it is—just whispers. Right now, nobody knows for sure what it means. But if there's a trial—I don't think I could stand it, Paul. I don't think I could stand it if all our friends and neighbors, if the people I work with, if the people who work for me, if they all knew. I couldn't stand it. I just couldn't."

My father is staring at her. So am I.

"Please, Paul," she says. "He's gone. Nothing is going to change that. Please."

It's quiet in the house. My mother is in her room. The door is closed. My father has gone out. He didn't say where he was going. He's been gone for hours. But before he left, I heard him make a phone call. I heard him say, "Detective, about that reward…"

I am lying on the couch in the family room. I wonder how long my mother has known about Danny. I wonder who told her. It wasn't my father and it wasn't me. Did Danny tell her? Did he get in trouble again and call her for help? Or did she find out by accident?

Sometimes she would go to Danny's place to drop off food for him—home-cooked meals. Sometimes when she was there, she tidied up the place for him. Did she find something or see something? Did she keep it to herself or did she talk to him about it? Did she make him promise not to tell my father, just like my father made him promise not to tell my mother? If that's what happened, was Danny proud of himself?

Scum

Was he proud of how much my parents loved him and how little he had to do to earn their love?

I think, if he were here now, I'd tell him how much I hate him. I'd tell him how stupid he is. And if he laughed at me the way he always did, I'd hit him. I'd hit him and hit him and hit him… Because there I was, telling Titch that whatever else he was, he was my brother and he was a good person. There I was, mad at Titch because he was lying to *me*. There I was, being a hypocrite.

After a while, I roll off the couch and hunt in the cupboard under the TV for the phone book. I look up the phone number for the bar where Titch works. I call and a man answers. It sounds like the bartender. I make my voice deeper so he won't know it's me. I ask for Titch. The bartender hangs up without saying another word. I call back. The phone rings into voice mail. I don't leave any message. I don't want to get Titch in trouble with the bartender. I try a few more times, hoping that Titch will answer. But every time I end up in voice mail.

When I come downstairs the next morning, my mother is dressed in the clothes she usually wears to work.

"I'm going to the office," she tells me.

"But it's Saturday." Sometimes my mother goes to the office on Saturday. Most of the time, she doesn't.

"I'm behind," she says. "I need to catch up."

"Where's Dad?"

"He went out."

"Where?"

"He didn't say."

"Did he say when he'll be back?"

She shakes her head. I have the feeling she didn't bother to ask him. I get a sick feeling in my stomach. After last night,

I wonder what is going to happen with my parents. My father can't stay in the spare room forever. I wonder if he will move back into the bedroom soon. If he doesn't, I wonder where he will go.

My mother leaves for the office. I go into the kitchen to get something to eat. I make tea and toast for myself, and I sit down at the table to eat. I flip through the TV listings. I flip through the fashion section. When I get up to put my dishes in the dishwasher, some of the newspaper falls onto the floor. I pick it up, and that's when I see it.

It isn't big.

It's one of those really short stories that they run along the side of the page. It's two short paragraphs. It says that someone was shot dead downtown last night. A kid. Anthony Pastorelli, known to his friends as Titch.

I stare at those two short paragraphs until the tears blind me.

Then I sink down onto the floor, and I sit there for what seems like forever. Titch is dead. Someone shot him.

I reach for the phone. I think of calling my mother. But she doesn't know Titch and she doesn't want to talk about what happened to Danny anymore. I think of calling my father instead. I start to punch in his cell phone number, but I don't finish. Instead I get up and pull Detective Rossetti's phone number off the fridge. While I am dialing, it occurs to me that maybe he won't answer. It's the weekend. Cops have days off, don't they?

But he does answer. He sounds surprised to hear that it's me. He sounds even more surprised when I tell him why I'm calling.

"I know him," I say.

"Was he a friend of yours?" Detective Rossetti says.

I say, "No." I explain how I met Titch. Then I ask him if he knows what happened.

"He was shot," Detective Rossetti says. "As far as we can tell, he died instantly."

"Do you know who did it?"

"He was shot in an alley a block from the bar where he worked," Detective Rossetti says. "So far we can't find anyone who heard or saw anything."

"What about the gun?" I say. I watch cop shows just like everyone else. "Was it the same gun that killed Danny?"

Detective Rossetti hesitates. Then he says, "No, it wasn't. Whoever killed Anthony left the gun right there. Probably whoever did it got the gun just to kill him. There's no prints. Nothing we can use. I'm sorry, Megan."

I don't know how I end up at the bar, but I do. When I get there, it's the middle of the afternoon. I open the door, half expecting the bouncer to block my way and tell me to get lost. But the bouncer isn't there. I walk right in. I look around and see there are maybe a dozen people scattered around the place, men mostly, drinking beer. I see the bartender behind the bar. He looks at me as I walk over to him.

"I heard about Titch," I say. "I heard what happened."

"You did, did you?" the bartender says. His voice is hard.

"I talked to the police. They said he was shot not far from here. You didn't hear anything?"

"I told you to stay out of here," the bartender says. "And I told him to stay away from you. But neither of you listened. You kept coming around. People saw you come around. They saw you pestering him. And now look."

I stare at him. "You think what happened to Titch is *my* fault?"

"I told you he didn't see what happened," the bartender says.

"But he did," I say. "He did see."

The bartender's face gets even harder. "Did he tell you that?"

I shake my head. "He didn't tell me anything. I just know it, that's all. I know he saw." He saw, and he was ashamed of himself that he saw and that he hadn't said anything. I don't know what else to say. I start to turn away.

"Hey," the bartender says. I turn back to face him. "Titch was a good kid," he says.

"I know."

"He didn't have any parents," the bartender says. "He didn't have a nice dad like you have. I bet you have a nice mom too. Titch didn't have that either. He had me. That's it. He worked hard. He was no genius, but he was doing okay in school. None of his teachers complained about him. He was going to graduate this spring, and then you know what he was going to do? He was going to try to get a job at one of those animal rescue places, you know, where they take in dogs that get abandoned or that were screwed up by their owners and they look after them? That's what he wanted to do. He wanted to look after animals."

"He wanted to get a dog."

"Yeah," the bartender says. "He wanted to get a dog. And what happens? Your brother happens, that's what. Your smartass brother. Thought pretty highly of himself. Thought he could take on anybody, anytime. Smart talker too. Always mouthing off to people. Well, you know what about your brother? He wasn't as smart as he thought he was. A nice kid like Titch is dead, and for what? For scum like your brother."

Scum

I feel myself shaking all over, but I don't say anything. I don't say anything at all. I walk out of the bar, and I take the bus home.

When I get there, I see that my father's car is in the driveway. I go into the house.

My father is in the kitchen. He's making spaghetti sauce. I see a loaf of Italian bread and a bulb of garlic. My father makes the best garlic bread I've ever tasted.

He smiles when he sees me. It isn't his usual thank-god-it's-Saturday-and-I-can-kick-back smile. This one is a tired smile. A sad smile.

"Your mother called," he says. "She won't be home for supper. But that doesn't mean we can't have a good meal, does it?"

I wonder if he knows about Titch. I wonder if I should tell him. I wonder what good it would do.

It's so quiet in the house.

I go over to the stove and sniff the sauce. I tell him it smells great. It really does. I say, "Is there anything I can do?"

My father's smile gets a tiny bit bigger. "You can make the salad," he says. Then he says, "I love you, Meggie."

orca soundings

For more information on all the books
in the Orca Soundings series, please visit
www.orcabook.com.

James C. Dekker is a first-time author and a fresh new voice in teen fiction. He lives in Toronto, Ontario, and, as far as he knows, is not known to police.